Glow in the Dark Trip to the Planets

Written by Lucille Hammond
Illustrated by Laurie Jordan

A GOLDEN BOOK • NEW YORK
Western Publishing Company, Inc., Racine, Wisconsin 53404

(See back cover for special Glow in the Dark directions!)

Title 1 Backpack

One spring morning Katie climbed into her spaceship and got ready for a long trip. She fastened all the safety buckles and checked all the switches. Then, after the countdown—10, 9, 8, 7, 6, 5, 4, 3, 2, 1, 0—she blasted off into the sky.

Soon she was orbiting Earth, and in no time at all, she had seen North America, South America, the Pacific Ocean, and the Atlantic Ocean. Now she could tell for sure that the world was really round.

Then Katie headed toward the moon. She traveled very fast and made a smooth landing when she got there.

Lucky Katie! She had lots of time to look around. She bounced along the cold and rocky surface in her space suit, and took many pictures on the way. She could see craters everywhere, and over the horizon, part of Earth appeared in the distance.

After her walk on the moon, Katie ate her delicious lunch and studied her map. She saw that there were nine planets: Mercury, Venus, Earth, Mars, Jupiter, Saturn, Uranus, Neptune, and Pluto.

Someday Katie hoped to visit all the planets. But now she was going to go to Mars. It was a long journey, so she had to make sure that everything was in order.

Earth

Jupiter

Mars was so far away that Katie slept for most of the trip. When she woke up, it was time to land.

"I am the first person to be on Mars," she exclaimed as she walked around. Everywhere she looked on the rugged surface she saw red dust. Now she knew why Mars was called the red planet.

Katie kept on exploring until it was time to go back to Earth. But then she had an idea.

"Now that I've come all this way," she thought, "why not go on to Jupiter and see the biggest planet of all?"

Once more Katie prepared to launch her spacecraft.

Off she flew. But, unfortunately, Katie had forgotten all about the asteroid belt between Mars and Jupiter. The big chunks of rock could easily bang into the spacecraft and damage it.

And suddenly, as Katie was speeding along in the direction of Jupiter, she found herself about to collide with an asteroid.

"Help!" she shouted, but there was no one to hear her, and she had to act quickly all by herself.

Right away Katie pulled a switch and avoided a disaster just in time.

Jupiter loomed in the distance. As Katie approached the planet she suddenly lost the power in her spacecraft. It went rolling and lunging in all directions. The lights went out and the spaceship turned upside down. Katie was terrified.

Jupiter

Earth

At that very moment Katie remembered the emergency power button which would direct the spacecraft toward Earth, using the engine's auxiliary power. It was her last chance! She pushed the button just in the nick of time. The spaceship immediately righted itself and raced back through the asteroid belt, past Mars, and toward Earth.

asteroid

When Katie was safely back on course, she relaxed and her heart stopped pounding. She began to enjoy herself again.

"I almost got to Jupiter," she said. "Next time I might make it!"

The return journey took a long time, but Katie dozed off now and then and began to dream. Sometimes she imagined what it would be like when she landed back on Earth.

She would be famous, she thought, and crowds of people would be there to greet her. They would shout, "Hurray for Katie! Hurray for Katie!"

When she woke up, Katie saw Earth in the distance. "My very own planet," thought Katie, and she gave a big sigh.

As she prepared for her landing Katie saw the Big Dipper and the Little Dipper.

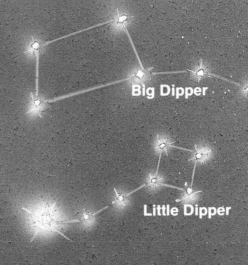

Big Dipper

Little Dipper

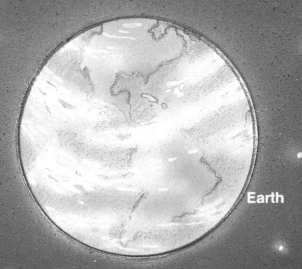

Earth

After a safe landing, Katie saw her father approaching the spaceship. He was smiling as he said, "What a good trip you had, Katie! Now it's time to go home."

And he helped her out of the spaceship.